One . . .
Two . . .
Three . . .

Stories in One

**Brigitta Gisella
Geltrich-Ludgate**

AuthorHouse™
1663 Liberty Drive
Bloomington, IN 47403
www.authorhouse.com
Phone: 833-262-8899

Because of the dynamic nature of the Internet, any web addresses or links contained in this book may have changed
since publication and may no longer be valid. The views expressed in this work are solely those of the author and do
not necessarily reflect the views of the publisher, and the publisher hereby disclaims any responsibility for them.

Any people depicted in stock imagery provided by Getty Images are models,
and such images are being used for illustrative purposes only.
Certain stock imagery © Getty Images.

This book is printed on acid-free paper.

ISBN: 978-1-6655-5975-1 (sc)
ISBN: 978-1-6655-5976-8 (hc)
ISBN: 978-1-6655-5974-4 (e)

Library of Congress Control Number: 2022909112

Print information available on the last page.

Published by AuthorHouse 05/19/2022

authorHOUSE

This book is dedicated to my grandmother,

Marta Marie Belser, the mother of my mother.

It is also dedicated to all the grandmothers who stepped out of the regular almost unseen grandmother role into a lively and modern grandmother.

CONTENTS

ONE . . .

Grandma then
and
Grandma now

Brigitta Gisella
Geltrich-Ludgate

Years ago, many years ago, at least fifty years ago or so, maybe even longer, Grandma was an old lady, dressed day in and day out in a long black dress, a kerchief on her thinning hair. Her dress almost touched the floor, and the long black sleeves of the dress covered halfway Grandma's gnarled hands. Her sparse hair tucked under a black kerchief was tied behind her neck in a knot. She usually sat somewhere in the back of a room. A heavy gnarled cane at her side or a walker, hand-made by one of the men in the household, possibly by one of grandma's sons, which aided her when she tried to get up and walk to somewhere. She was no longer secure on her feet. She hardly got out of the chair to use the cane or the walker, only when her bedtime came and her daughter or her daughter-in-law took her out of the room. Grandma was old then, an old woman and everyone was hoping that she will pass on soon and the house and the land on which the house stood will become theirs. Grandma was in her sixties, maybe in her seventies, hardly ever in her early eighties. She had little to say in the household anymore, if anything, even though the house was hers and the land it stood on was hers. Both had been taken away from her years ago. She had been relegated to a corner in a room, often sitting on a creaky old chair or in an old rocking chair, which no longer rocked much, and mumbling something which no one understood unless they came up to her really close, putting their ears to her quivering lips. But no one actually came up to her, not close enough to put their ears against her lips. At least not the adults in the family did so, and so her mouth was going all the time. Maybe she moved it in the hope that someone would come and listen to what she had to say. Most likely there was still a lot she wanted to say.

It was different with the children. Grandma had a lot to say when a grandchild came up to her and begged her to tell a story. Grandma's stories were always of the old time when Grandma was young. But she never let on to the children that the young, beautiful girl in the story she was talking about had been she. She left that identification up to the children. Sometimes they got it, most of the times they did not.

"Once upon a time . . .," Grandma always started her stories, "there was a beautiful girl which grew into a beautiful lady." Grandma always ended her story with "they lived happily ever after." But when the children left, Grandma mumbled to herself, "if they did. Most of the times they did not live happily ever after. At least one of them did not." There were tears in Grandma's eyes. No one saw the tears. At least not the adults. No one asked why Grandma was crying.

Today, Grandma is in her eighties, or nineties, some even in their hundreds. She is still spry. She hardly ever uses a cane or a walker. She runs her own house, takes care of Grandpa, if he is still alive, and if he is, once a year she goes on a cruise with him, partaking in all sorts of shore excursions. Her clothes are colorful and modern. She wears even slacks and tunics. Grandma's hair is either curly framing her face or it is hanging down to her shoulders or it is combed in an elegant upsweep. She has no time to sit in a corner of a room or rocking in an old chair, which really hardly ever rocks, her lips moving in an almost silent speech, waiting for the children to come to her begging her for a story. Grandma has other things to do.

"Do you want to go to the carnival?" she asks instead, standing in front of the children. Exuberantly the youngsters answer, "Yes." And off Grandma drives the car to a grand day at the carnival or at the zoo, or to a boat ride to watch the numerous sea animals or river animals coming up to the surface curiously watching who is there, begging for food, at least they are begging for recognition and possibly for a friendly pat.

Nowadays, Grandma's life is in the midst of the family, living by herself, enjoying every minute of it, visiting her children and their children a few times the year, each time bringing something to the little ones, a tiny toy or a piece of candy, or something like that. After the visit, Grandma drives her own car home and enjoys her life even though Grandpa might have been gone for quite a while. Grandma feels young, and she is young. She is determined. No one tells her that she is old, after all, grandma is not old. Age is just a mere number, nothing else.

TWO . . .

Why Was the Sun Hiding?

Brigitta Gisella
Geltrich-Ludgate

That was the most unusual thing that ever happened. It happened way up in the sky. It also happened down here on Earth and to some extent on all the other planets of our galaxy. It is hard to believe. It all had to do with the sun. Mr. Sun was suddenly fearful. He wanted to hide. Completely hide. Be out of sight. Not be seen by anybody.

"Let me stay here," Mr. Sun shouted completely breathlessly.

He stood in front of an old red barn with some of the siding loose. The Sun was so large, it covered almost the entire barn doors. Of course, that is much smaller than when Mr. Sun was up in the sky. There he was tremendously large. He was tremendously huge. There was nothing in comparison that large here on Earth. But Mr. Sun could adjust. He could make himself smaller. And that is what he had done. He was quite small in comparison to his normal self.

"I need to hide," Mr. Sun said, still out of breath.

A little boy looked as much as it was possible for him to look straight at the Sun. The Sun was rather bright and hurt the little boy's eyes.

"Why?" the little boy asked, looking at the Sun through his spread fingers which were covering his eyes.

"I must hide," said the Sun.

With those words the Sun slipped into the barn and pulled the barn door shut behind him. It was no longer bright outside the barn. The little boy removed his fingers from his eyes. There were just a few beams coming through the loose boards of the barn. They were not as bright as the full Sun seemed to have been only moments ago and particularly not as bright as when the Sun stands in the sky. They were actually diminishing in their brightness.

With it, it grew dark outside the barn, and it grew cold. A fierce wind started up and blew relentlessly around the barn building and rattled the red barn door. The entire barn was in motion. But Mr. Sun did not open the barn doors to let the wind in, nor did Mr. Sun come out of the barn. The wind reluctantly shook its head and withdrew from the barn and disappeared.

The little boy started to shiver as he looked at some narrow beams of the Sun which were penetrating the gaps of the barn slabs. Those beams were warm and the little boy stood in them to keep warm himself. But the beams were losing their warmness. Their brightness was diminishing more and more as well.

"Bobby," called the boy's mother from the house. "Something is wrong with the Sun. It seems to have disappeared. Maybe it is hiding behind the clouds. But . . . but why is it so dark and why is it so cold?" The mother stood on the verandah, looking straight up into the sky. "The Sun seems to be nowhere up there," she said.

Bobby left the warmth of the sunbeams which came through the loose slabs of the barn and ran to the house. He clutched his shoulders as he felt the coldness once again penetrating him.

"Did you see what happened?" The mother asked as she took Bobby inside the house.

Bobby sort of nodded. It was a meek nod. He had seen something but was not quite sure of what he had seen. The Sun had slipped into the barn and had not come out of the barn again. That was something unusual. Bobby had never seen something like that before. He was not sure whether his mother was going to believe him. He stuttered to her, "The Sun is hiding in the barn."

The mother looked at Bobby in great disbelief. Why would the Sun hide in the barn, in their old red barn? The dilapidated old barn? The mother shook her head. She did not believe Bobby.

Now why did the Sun hide in that old almost broken down barn? The old red barn of Bobby's father's farm? Was he afraid of something outside the barn? But why would he be afraid? He was such a powerful thing of the sky. The most powerful thing in the sky and on earth. Actually, the most powerful thing in the whole galaxy. He should not be afraid. But the Sun seemed to be afraid, terribly afraid.

Well, it was the disastrous behavior of the Moon that had made the Sun to be suddenly so fearful. But the Moon was such a tiny thing in the sky in comparison to the Sun. What was the Sun afraid of? After all, the Sun was so much larger than the Moon. It was even larger than the Earth around which the Moon circulated. And the moon was small in comparison to the Earth. That is quite strange. The Sun had a lot more power than that tiny bit of power the Moon held. Everyone in the Sun's circle of friends knew that the Earth was not very large. It was just one of eight planets which circulated around the Sun in order to absorb some of the Sun's warmth and its light.

The Earth was just a mere blue bauble, and the Moon was not even visible from anywhere in space. It was so tiny. Each of the other planets, almost all of them had moons, some had even more than one moon. So why would that tiny Moon of the Earth suddenly exert such power over the Sun, making the Sun completely fearful, so fearful that he needed to look for a hiding place? So terribly fearful that the Sun had slipped into Bobby's father's barn to get away from things, particularly from the Moon. Now what gave the Moon such power? What did the Moon think the Sun was? Better yet, what did the Moon think she was?

Well now, the Moon had sort of a size complex or was it being a brightness complex. She felt proud of being the only satellite of the Earth and brightening that blue bauble up during the night. She did not have to compete with other moons. She was the only one around Earth. That was something to be proud of. And she was proud of shining most brightly almost every night that is if the night sky was clear of clouds or along sea coasts clear of marine layers. And when the night sky was clear of clouds and there was no marine layer sweeping in onto the land from the open sea, the Moon shone a bright light down on Earth. Even during daytime when it was the time for the Sun to shine and the Moon to rest, the Moon was still in the sky, not at all asleep what she was supposed to be doing.

What the Moon did not like was to be at times a mere sliver one way or the other, facing either left or right. It was the mere sliver which upset the Moon the most. She knew that it had something to do with the Earth being in between her and the Sun. The Sun was never a sliver. That was annoying as well. The Moon wanted to be round and bright all the time, and if possible, the Moon wanted to have her own furnace with which to keep the Earth warm. But Mr. Sun was always interfering with the Moon being round and bright at all times and sending warm beams toward Earth. It was exasperating. Something had to be done about the Sun. And it had to be done fast. Very fast! The Moon had to get higher up in the sky than the Sun was. That was for sure. Then she could exude her power over the Sun.

The Moon was fully aware that it was up to her to do that something that changed the situation.

And that something was to hover between the Earth and the Sun, and since the Moon was just the right size, distance wise, she covered the entire Sun every day and it was dark down on the Earth. Only bright enough as the shining of moonbeams allowed it to be. That was a great trick the Moon played. She felt she was in control. In control over the Sun. It was effective. No matter how much the Sun moved this way or that way, to the right or to the left or up or down, the Moon was always between him and the Earth.

"Come on now," the Sun said. "You are upsetting part of the global roles."

"Ha!" snickered the Moon.

"Come on now. I should be shining during the day," said the Sun.

"You stay wherever I want you to stay," commanded the Moon.

"But you're hiding me."

"Exactly, that is what I want."

The Moon laughed the loudest laugh. It was such an unladylike behavior, but the Moon did not care. "And if you don't stay, I will send a sharp dart your way. It will pierce you and you will deflate where it hits you and lose your brightness there." With that the Moon moved up above the Sun somewhat more. The Sun was suddenly hanging below the Moon. That was a dangerous position to be in, but that was exactly where the Moon wanted the Sun to be. Below him. That made the Sun powerless. At least powerless over the moon.

The Moon sent a rather sharp dart down to the Sun. It hit her right in the chin. It hurt the Sun something fierce. What was worse was that where the dart had hit the Sun, the light of the Sun went out and there was a dark hollow in the Sun's chin.

The Sun was deflating something fast where the dart had hit him. The Sun let out a moan. He was in pain. The dart had hurt him something terribly.

The Sun was in desperate need of a doctor and really fast. That was for sure. But there was no doctor in the sky or, for that matter, in the entire universe. The only doctors, as the Sun knew it, were down on the Earth, and that is why the Sun limped down to the Earth when the Moon was busy jubilating her success. The Sun reached the Earth right in front of Bobby's father's old red barn. *Why not hide in that barn*, the Sun thought, *as I wait for the doctor?*

"Little boy," Mr. Sun called as Bobby ran toward the house. "I need to ask you for some help."

But Bobby did not hear Mr. Sun. He was inside the house trying to explain to his mother what has happened to the Sun. *I need a doctor*, the Sun mumbled. *Is anyone listening? I am in great pain.*

It did not take long for the Moon, up in the sky, to realize that the Sun was no longer shining down on Earth and as a matter of fact down on all of the other planets. To be exact, the Sun was not anywhere. Now where could Mr. Sun have gone to? The Moon evidently had not been keeping an eye on the Sun too much after shooting the dart at him. Did she lose control over the Sun? She started to look for him everywhere. She looked here and she looked there and she looked everywhere in the sky, and nowhere could she see Mr. Sun. Had that huge disk, which the Moon was trying to overpower, overpowered her? Had that huge disk won the battle? The Moon was truly upset, at least she was concerned about her powers. With Mr. Sun being nowhere, and the Moon wondering where he might be, the Moon started to feel her own powers slipping away. Actually, the Moon's brightness was dissipating rather rapidly as well. It was downright unexplainable what was happening.

Well, with the Sun hiding in the red barn of Bobby's father, things on Earth started to change as well. It was suddenly perpetually dark. There was no more sunshine besides the few beams which penetrated through the loose slabs of the barn but their brightness seemed to diminish rather rapidly. Everyone was affected by these changes, mostly by the darkness. The people lost control over when it was time for them to go to bed and to sleep and when it was time for them to get up and go to work, the animals slept all the time. They just did not want to get up. Why should they? There was nothing for them to do or for that matter for many of them to see. The farmers could not work on their fields. No seed sprouted. Not a single plant grew. Not even the weeds grew. And how about the weather?

Well now, the weather was something else. There were no solar winds anymore, there were no winds at all. There were no more clouds in the sky than there were when Mr. Sun looked for shelter inside that old red barn. There were no storms, there was nothing of what had been when the Sun was standing high above the Earth. It was a disaster down on Earth. Everything seemed to stand still and mostly, everything was surrounded by coldness. Actually it was getting colder with every minute the Sun was no longer there sending its warming beams comfortably down to Earth.

Bobby's mother did not believe what Bobby had been telling her. How could Mr. Sun, that humongous disk of the sky, of the entire galaxy, hide inside the red barn? The red barn was not that large. It actually was rather tiny. A puny little thing in comparison to Mr. Sun. Mr. Sun was humongously large when he stood in the sky. He must have been completely outsizing the barn when he was down on Earth.

"Come on, now, Bobby," the mother said.

"Come and see for yourself," Bobby said, tugging on his mother's arm. He reached for her hand and rather reluctantly the mother followed him. The two of them walked down the slope toward the barn. From a distance they could hear a loud sobbing. It got louder and louder, extremely loud when they came closer to the barn. And by the quivering of the narrow sunbeams penetrating the loose barn slabs, Bobby's mother soon realized that the sobs came from something large hiding inside the barn. As far as Bobby was concerned, it was the Sun. The Sun seemed to be rather upset.

"What is the matter, Mr. Sun?" Bobby asked.

"I am hurting something really badly," Mr. Sun said, "where the Moon had shot one of her fierce darts into me. I have quite a wound there."

"Maybe we need to get Dr. Frank from town to tend to your wound," said Bobby's mother.

The Sun stopped sobbing. He was all for it to have a doctor check his wound. The pain was excruciating.

And so Dr. Frank came to the old red barn. He had been told by Bobby's mother that the patient was a rather unusual patient and that he needed to put on a heavy pair of sunglasses. Dr. Frank was not sure whether he could see the wound the patient had, at least details of the wound through a pair of sunglasses. The sunglasses would most definitely hinder him from doing so. But he nonetheless brought a pair along with him.

"You must turn down your light," said Bobby to Mr. Sun and Mr. Sun did just that. He left a tiny bit of light for the doctor to see the wound and to tend to it. The doctor gave the Sun an antibiotic injection and covered the wound with a large bedsheet to protect it from the dirt inside the old red barn.

"He needs to rest for a while," said Dr. Frank. "Just fluff up the hay for him in which he lies." Bobby's mother nodded. She will do just that.

"I will help," said Bobby.

The mother hugged Bobby.

And so Mr. Sun lay back and went to sleep. The medication was rather effective. The deeper he slept the less the beams were shining. It was getting dark inside the barn as well. It was very dark outside the barn. It was downright unbelievably dark all around the galaxy. The Sun had never before fallen asleep. But this time, he had. He was sound asleep.

Up in the sky, there was a lot of commotion. The Moon rushed all over the heavens looking for the Sun. She could not find him. As she hurried, her light got dimmer and dimmer. Almost all of the brightness was going out. "What am I going to do without any light?" The Moon asked. She looked down to Earth. Earth was dark as well. There was no day time or dawn time or dusk time. There was only nighttime. Everywhere nighttime. Even way out in the galaxy there was nighttime. All the planets were draped in total darkness. The Moon stood there scratching her head. "What is happening?" she asked. "It usually is so bright."

Well now, the Moon just did not realize that all the light had come from one source, namely from Mr. Sun, and Mr. Sun was sound asleep inside the barn.

Dr. Frank came twice more to Bobby's father's farm to check on his patient inside the red barn. Each time he removed the large bedsheet from the wound and replaced it with a new bedsheet. The wound started to heal. It was crusting over. Mr. Sun was feeling better. He no longer sobbed. He actually sat up and looked around.

"This is quite a place," he said. He seemed to appreciate the red barn. "It is safe in here."

"Now he needs to get strong again," said Dr. Frank. He turned toward the Sun. "No getting out of the hay and walking around. You need to eat and getting stronger. Do some exercises and be a good patient."

The sun nodded. He will be a good patient.

And Bobby's mother responded with a lot of good and healthy food and Bobby responded with a lot of exercises, from tiny ones to ever so demanding ones, all the while the sun was sitting in his bed in the hay.

Slowly the Sun was getting stronger and slowly the light shining through the slabs of the old red barn grew brighter, even through the large bedsheet which covered the wound the beams grew brighter. The light grew so bright that the Moon up on a cloud bench noticed it.

"Wait a second," she said. "What is that?"

There was a bright beam of something shining all the way up into the sky where the Moon was. "Could that be the Sun?" asked the Moon. "Is the Sun hiding down on Earth?"

The Moon hurried down to Earth in the direction of the beam that had alerted her that the Sun might be down there. The Moon in its large size stopped in front of the old red barn and looked at the bright beam that was shining through the broken down slaps of the barn.

"Is that you, Sun?" the Moon asked.

The Sun did not respond.

"Only you can have such a bright gleam," said the Moon.

The Sun still did not say anything. An answer came from Bobby instead.

"Get away," Bobby's voice ordered.

The boy had come running from his house, when he saw that huge disk of the moon rolling in from the sky. He momentarily stopped as he saw the Moon standing in front of the barn. It was a rather large disk in comparison to him and to the barn. But Bobby felt he needed to protect Mr. Sun and continued running toward the old red barn.

"Get away from there," Bobby shouted, furiously swinging his arms up and down, touching somewhat the Moon, trying to push her away.

The Moon turned around and her very weak glow covered Bobby. It was so weak, Bobby could look right into it. He did not need his fingers to cover his eyes.

"You are not wanted here," Bobby shouted.

Before the Moon could answer, there was a huge banging coming from the inside of the old red barn. It sounded like someone was trying to break down the barn doors. The Moon turned around to look at the barn. No one broke down the doors, but the banging continued.

"What is that?" the Moon asked.

Bobby did not answer.

The banging continued. It actually grew louder and louder. It turned ear shatteringly loud.

As the Moon turned around to look at Bobby, Bobby shouted at the barn, hoping Mr. Sun will hear him, "Run!"

There was another banging at the old red barn doors. With a tremendous crash, the barn doors broke open and scattered all around the entrance. Mr. Sun came out in a running speed, right past the Moon, who sort of had fallen back when he had heard the crashing of the doors and had heard the rushing feet of Mr. Sun. Pieces of wood splinters flew all around Mr. Sun and settled down on the Moon.

Mr. Sun stopped quite a distance away from the Moon. There he turned around. He was hanging in the air a bit higher than the Moon. Mr. Sun knew that the Moon could not shoot another dart at him, because she was hanging so much lower than he was. A celestial being can only shoot downward. That was some kind of galactic rule, and the Sun knew it.

"So, what's the matter with you?" the Sun asked. "You seemed to be speechless."

"I'll shoot another dart in you," the Moon shouted.

"You will not be able to do that?"

"How come?" the Moon wanted to know.

"You are no longer above me and cannot shoot at me as I am hovering higher in the sky than you do."

"We'll see about that," said the Moon.

With every effort the Moon made to rise higher than the Sun, to stand above him to shoot another arrow at Mr. Sun, she was unsuccessful. The Sun was strong enough by now to get a bit higher with every move the Moon made. Finally the Moon fell back. She was exhausted. She realized, she could not climb higher than the Sun anymore.

"Had enough?" Mr. Sun asked, growing larger and larger and brighter and brighter as he spoke.

The Moon did not respond.

"Now, let's talk," said Mr. Sun. He pulled up a cloud and sat down on it. He still needed a bit of rest, maybe even some support of his once aching body. Sitting down on a cloud seemed to be just the right thing for him to do. He patted the cloud, letting the Moon know to sit down as well.

And so the Sun and the Moon had a talk as they sat on a couple of fluffy clouds. Actually the Sun had a good talk with the Moon. It was a lengthy talk and it took the Sun quite a while to have the Moon understand each of their set roles in the sky. Those were roles established a long time ago, possibly at the beginning of the galaxy. Possibly when the Sun was born. The moon could not change them, even though if she wanted to do that, and the Sun could not change them even though he did not want to do that.

"I will shine at day time," started the Sun, "and you will shine at nighttime."

The Moon listened.

"I will be bright during the day time and you will be bright at night time."

The Moon nodded slightly.

"I have my place in the vast galaxy," the Sun said "and you will have your place around the Earth."

The Moon looked at the Sun.

"Your place will always be around the Earth, nowhere else," said the Sun.

The moon nodded rather slowly. That was hard to swallow. It was rather constraining, she thought.

"And my place will be the center of our galaxy," the Sun continued, "nowhere else."

The Moon was silent. She liked that Mr. Sun was also being constrained.

"Is that understood?" the Sun asked.

Since the Sun was so enormously large by now and the Moon was so exremely small, so tiny, the Moon had no other choice than to agree. It was hard to understand what the Sun had said, but the Moon had to understand. Her place was nowhere else than circling around the Earth and not even that. The Moon could only circle the Earth one sided. Her backside never got to face the Earth. That was embarrassingly sad. The Sun's place was the center of the galaxy. That was great for him but not for the Moon.

"Without my light and my warmth," the Sun continued, "you cannot exist."

That put the scare into the Moon. She wanted so much to exist and so she agreed with the Sun, no matter what the consequences might be.

And so, the Sun is the center of the galaxy and will send her light and warmth to all the planets in the galaxy, even to Earth and to the Moon that circles the Earth. Actually the Sun will be sending his warmth and his light to the Earth and the Earth will reflect both to the Moon.

What a blow! The Moon hung her head.

For years now, the Moon has been circulating around the Earth ever since with only one side visible, and the Sun has been sending his light and his warmth down to Earth ever since as well. And the Earth has been reflecting her light and her warmth to the Moon. At least so it is believed by the Moon. The Moon is thankful to the Earth and a tiny bit she is thankful to the Sun. Deep down so, the Moon was scheming how to get both of her sides facing the Earth by turning around herself, and from there, there would be better things to come for the Moon. She would at least have regained some power. And power was all what she wanted.

Let us wait and see if that ever happens. Do you believe it will?

THREE . . .

The Skyscraper With Wheels

Brigitta Gisella
Geltrich-Ludgate

Have you ever heard of a skyscraper having wheels, just like a pushcart or shopping cart or any other cart? Well the skyscraper I am going to tell you about has wheels on either of its bottom right sides. Two large wheels, each about four stories high and covering four windows across. The skyscraper stands there among other skyscrapers looking like being ready to be pushed away, to somewhere else, possibly to a better location. Who knows?

That is what I saw when I left the taxi in front of the hotel. The hotel was actually two skyscrapers built side by side, both being attached to one another. One skyscraper is large, the other is somewhat smaller. The hotel must have a lot of customers checking in in order to use two skyscrapers. I stood outside the hotel and stared at the wheels, as the doorman tried to wheel my suitcase inside.

"Are you coming lady?" he asked.

I did not respond.

"Don't you want to check in?"

Of course, I wanted to check in. I was just mesmerized to see the two wheels. *Are they functional? Will the hotel wheel away when I am asleep?* I was a bit hesitant to follow the doorman, but I finally did and stood in front of the check in with my passport and credit card in hand.

"That's quite a hotel," I mentioned.

"Indeed it is," said the check-in clerk. "We are rather proud of it."

As soon as I had taken my suitcase up to the room, my home away from home for a couple of nights, I went back down to the lobby and rushed outside of the hotel. Yes, indeed, it had a huge wheel at the side of the larger building. The shorter building was up front. Way up on top of the larger skyscraper there was a lookout platform. It was a covered one and towered over the tops of nearby skyscrapers with its height of forty-three stories. It seemed to hover there, like a UFO and had numerous windows through which one could look out over the city and beyond. *What could one see*, I thought, *if the wheels started moving and took the two skyscrapers to another location?* I wondered. It must be a lot more to see wherever the skyscraper was going to wheel to. But how does one wheel a skyscraper from one spot to another spot? The two buildings were rather large and they must be rather heavy. But the wheels on either side of the larger building were also rather large. They possibly could carry the two skyscrapers. With no answer given me, I slowly went back inside the hotel and up to my room. I shook my head. I just could not believe it that the hotel could be pushed away.

The thought did not leave me. I could not stay very long in my room. I was just too mesmerized by the two attached skyscrapers and the two wheels. I went back outside and stood in front of this dual skyscraper, not really knowing what to do next, particularly with those two humongous wheels at the bottom of one of them. All I could do was asking myself, *what is the purpose of these wheels? What is the purpose of the skyscraper with wheels?* I had never seen something like that before. *What is it all about? Do the wheels really work? Do they really move? Can they really push two skyscrapers?* I had many questions. *Can they really move the skyscraper to somewhere else? To another location? Maybe a better location?* I gave the wheels a try to push them but was not strong enough to give the wheels an initial shove to get the skyscrapers moving. I was just a short human being. Being a mere five foot five and there was no one around me to give those wheels of the larger skyscraper a shove to get them rolling. All the hotel people were helping customers and had no time to talk to me or to push the wheels, if the wheels could actually be pushed.

I asked some of the people who rushed past me, but they were in such a hurry, they did not hear my question. Or they just did not know my language. Or they just had no answer. Or they did not know what I was talking about.

I was in a rich Asian country at a conference. The people were surrounded by a lot of interesting skyscrapers, one with wheels meant little if not anything to them. I also did not speak the language of the people and they acted as if they did not hear me. We just did not communicate with one another. We did not connect. Evidently, to the people, all the skyscrapers in their city were of different build. If need be every single one of them needed answers to the questions by visitors to their city. *Who, what, when, where?* The locals did not have time to do just that. So, they ignored me and offered no answer.

I walked around the two skyscrapers looking for a button or a handle with which to operate the wheels, to set them in motion. Maybe they just span around to the enjoyment of children. But there was nowhere a button or a handle to push or to pull down. I had to resign myself to the fact that the two wheels were just an illusion. Just a mere decoration. They really were not operative. Even though they looked like they could be. They were just built into the building for the enjoyment of children, and for the grownups to start them to think. I certainly was thinking. The symbols on the wheels on either site spelled GFG. *Could that be the initials of the building?* I thought. *Could they be of the builder?* I decided that most likely they were the initials of the builder. Or were they of something else? Who knows. Maybe I needed to find the builder and hope the builder had the initials GFG. But where will I look to find the builder.

Being convinced that the two wheels were not functional, I went back inside the hotel and rode the elevator up to the level where my room was located. It was not until later that day that I decided to explore the larger building. I always did that whenever I was staying at a hotel in a strange city. I used to get to see a lot of the town and its suburbs, particularly from the top floors. I decided to take the elevator to the top floor of the hotel. I had spent some time on the street level at the double skyscrapers wondering about the wheels. Maybe there might be more information about them at the platform of the larger building.

There was a bank of elevators at each side of the elevator hall. I concentrated on those elevators with the arrow pointing up. It seemed to be that two of the elevators just had these going up symbols. They went straight up to the observation platform, bypassing all other floors. It was an enormous speed with which the elevator zapped me up from the fifth-level floor to the forty-third floor. I had to repeatedly clear my ears for fear if I do not do it that I will get deaf. On the forty third floor the elevator stopped. The doors silently opened and I found myself on that satellite-looking platform observation deck I had already seen from the street level. I stood there for a moment in front of the elevator door to get my balance back and then I headed straight out onto the platform that lead around the entire deck. The platform appeared to be moving, not fast though, but it was definitely moving in one direction, going clockwise.

In the center of the platform, next to the elevators, there rose shops, all kinds of shops, gift shops and food stands. The aroma of the food was enticing. I felt pangs of hunger in my stomach, but was certain to give the observation deck a chance first what sights it had to offer me and possibly an answer about the wheels before I took care of the gnawing pangs of my stomach.

Looking out of the windows, which ran around the entire platform, I had a view over the whole city along with its suburbs, a view of old houses and new houses, of old squares and new squares, of narrow streets and broad streets and of what not else was everywhere, and in between the blocks of houses and streets there were large green parks with wide open spaces. They were presumably there for people to sit together and chat or eat or for people to sunbathe or for areas where to kick balls or whip their whips or doing exercises, whatever the people do on open places in that country. After I had looked out of almost every second or third window skirting the platform, time must have passed. It had gone by rather fast. I looked around me and the gift shops and the food stands were closing for the day. My gnawing stomach had to wait until I was back on the ground level of the hotel where I had my room, looking for a restaurant there.

To get down, I was searching for an elevator with the symbol pointing downward and take me to the street level. I finally found it at the bank of elevators on the opposite side from where I had come up. There were a lot of buttons in all colors waiting to be pushed at this side of elevators. They were pointing in every direction except for going upward. They must be leading to individual levels including the one where I wanted to get off. I pushed the one that went straight down, so the symbol on it indicated. None of the elevator doors opened. I pushed the one with the symbol pointing left. Nothing happened. I pushed the button with the symbol pointing right. Still nothing. Panic set in. I wanted to get off the platform and ride safely down to the street level. But as the nonfunctioning elevator buttons informed me, I was going to evidently spend the night on the platform. That was something I did not want to do. I slammed my hand at several buttons at the same time. There was a green flash and a mechanical bang. It sounded like I wanted to start a car on a cold morning and could not get it going. And then I felt it. It was a rather strange sensation.

The building started to weave backward a bit under my feet. And then it weaved forward a bit. I felt like I needed to hold onto something not to fall. It was as if someone was pushing the building. The floor was slanted, down toward the right. I crawled up toward the windows to look out. And there I saw the skyscrapers around the two of them I was currently on fall back and the two skyscrapers I was on were moving forward until they came to the park, the furthest away green spot I had seen, and there they stopped, straightened out, and one of the elevator doors opened up allowing me to get on the elevator and ride to the street level. But it was not a street level where the elevator landed. It was in the middle of the park. I stood there staring at the greenness around me, the green trees around me, the green grass, the green bushes, the green plants around me. Everything was green. The children around me wore green clothes, the men wore green suits, and the women wore green pants and green tops. All their faces were green, their hands were green. Some did not wear shoes, which in all instances were green, and their feet were green. Their hair was green. It all smelled like freshly moved grass. I closed my eyes and shook my head. When I opened my eyes, everything around me was still green. Lawnmowers of all shapes and sizes stood everywhere. Every single one was green, all shades of green, and if they were not pushed by the green people, they ran by themselves being careful not to run into each other.

It was a strange world in which I found myself, and the hope suddenly came up in my mind that if I pushed other buttons up on the skyscraper platform I will see other worlds. Maybe nicer worlds and not green worlds. But first I had to find the elevator. For the time being, it was nowhere in sight. Nor were the dual skyscrapers.

"Where are your green clothes," a lawnmower type of voice rattled from behind me.

"You do know you have to wear green clothes," another voice crackled.

"You can't walk around here in our green world the way you are dressed," still another voice called from somewhere.

"So go home and change," they all seemed to agree. I could have sworn that the lawnmowers momentarily stopped mowing and nodded their agreement.

"I do not have a home here," I responded softly, almost fearfully of all that racket around me.

"No green clothes?" the first voice rattled.

"No green clothes."

"What about your face and hair and hands, possibly your feet?" the second voice crackled.

"I do not know how to get them green."

"Then you better run away from our peaceful green world, because the verdant police will come and will lock you up. And . . ."

"And?" I asked.

"The lawnmowers will run over you one by one until you are gone."

As the lawnmowers circled in on me and in the distance the sirens of the verdant police were howling, I started to run. I ran and I ran. But where could I run to? I had to find the dual skyscrapers with the elevators, but it was nowhere, no matter where I looked.

I called for it as I ran. It did not come. I whistled for it, slowing down in my speed. It did not come. I finally stopped running and lowered myself onto the green grass and lamented, "Dear elevator, I really need you. Please come," and with a strange noise, almost a cracking bang, the enormous skyscraper dual stood in front of me and one of the upward going elevator doors stood wide open. I did not hesitate whatsoever to rush into the open elevator. The doors immediately closed behind me. In no time I was back up on the platform and in front of the elevator button bank with the multitude of buttons. "Which one should I push now?" I asked myself. "I need to get down to the street level."

My hand moved toward the button clearly marked with an F. It was there all by itself. "Why not," I said and pushed the button. The same thing happened as before.

The building weaved backward and forward under my feet, and then tilted as it moved closer to the center of town. But it did not go all the way to the center where the dual skyscrapers belonged. It stopped at one of the green parks. It opened the elevator door and literally spewed me out. I found myself in a gulley of another green park. As I looked around, the skyscrapers were gone.

For a moment, I closed my eyes. I did not want to see anything anymore that was green. As I slightly opened my eyes, nothing around me was green. But the houses looked like temples and mosques and churches and cathedrals, and small chapels. All of them hanging precariously on the slopes of the gulley. Everywhere were these houses of worship. And the people walking around everywhere wore long gowns, white ones, black ones, even colored ones. Even the children wore these gowns.

"Where on earth am I now?" I said to myself.

A small boy came up to me and touched my slacks.

"What are these?" he asked.

"They are slacks," I answered.

"What are they for?"

"They are my clothes."

I knew I should not have said that.

A chorus of voices chanted around me, sounding much like monks in their monasteries. "Those cannot be clothes in our world. So, take them off."

Before I could respond with that they were clothes, a man dressed in snow white and a turban wrapped around his head stepped up to me and asked me what faith I was.

"Faith?" I asked.

"Yes, to what faith do you belong?"

I had to think about what the best answer might be, but the man and those following him in their long robes started to shout for their faithful police.

"We have an interloper here," they shouted, "who does not know to what faith he belongs."

Out of the corner of my eyes I saw a police car approaching. I started to run, faster and faster all the while I shouted, "Skyscrapers."

But the skyscrapers did not come.

"Please, skyscrapers come."

Before I knew it I was back on the forty third floor of the larger skyscraper taken there by the elevators.

"I will not push a button again," I said to myself and went to look for the staircase which will bring me all the way down to the street level. But there was nowhere a door with the Exit sign above it and stairs behind it that will take me to the street level. I was dependent on the elevator buttons.

When I turned around to look at the bank of elevator buttons, there was only one button on the entire elevator wall. It spelled out "G."

Now what does "G" stand for I asked myself. It certainly could not be *Green*. I was already where everything was green.

I had no time to wait for an answer even if there had been an answer available to me. The elevator doors opened and someone pushed me inside whether I wanted to go inside or not. As the elevator door slid to a close behind me and the elevator started to rock and then to move, the entire skyscraper began to move, leaning back at first, then forward and it did not stop moving until it was in the green park not far away from where the skyscrapers home base was. The doors sprang wide open and someone pushed me outside. I could not even consider on my own whether to go outside the elevator or not. Behind me, the elevator doors closed with a loud thud, and then the dual skyscrapers vanished, elevator and all.

I stood there on the grass of this new park. It was neither green nor was it brown. It was sort of yellowish. There was no one around, no people, no children, no animals, nothing at all. No trees, no bushes, no plants, absolutely nothing. The only thing I saw was in the far off distance. It was a huge greyish board with some writing on it. The board was too far off. I could not read the writing. I walked toward it. It was a lengthy walk. Every time I thought I had reached the board, it was even further away.

I must have walked a whole day and still had not reached the greyish board. I was getting tired. I wanted to lie down and sleep. My legs were aching. But when I tried to lie down, someone pulled me back up on my feet and pushed me forward. It was not until evening came that I reached the greyish board. There was one sentence on the board.

"What is your goal?" the sentence asked.

I had no idea what my goal was. All I wanted to do was to present my paper at the conference and attend other presentations. The words on the board changed to "What is your goal for the future?"

I was thinking. I had to have a goal. But what was it? I want to be . . .to be a . . . I closed my eyes as I thought.

When I opened my eyes again, I lay on top of the bed in my hotel room. The curtains were still open. It was dark outside. I was fully clothed. Even had my shoes on. I must have fallen asleep.

I sat at the edge of the bed and shook my head. "Was that all a dream?" I asked. "What a strange dream that was."

I got up from the bed and walked to the door. I went outside and looked for the elevators. One of them waited with wide-open doors at my level. The arrow above the elevator pointed down. I entered it and went down to the street level. I rushed through the lobby to the large glass doors and went outside. There I stood, looking at the two skyscrapers. They were there. One taller than the other. But when I looked where the wheels had been, I could not find them. They were no longer there.

Now why did I have such a dream? I could not understand it. Maybe I should have cut the lawn around my house before I left. That would explain the dream of green, but how about the dream of faith and the dream of goal. I had to think about it quite some more. I just do not understand those two parts of the dream.

Do you understand them?

LIST OF BOOKS BY THE AUTHOR

Brigitta Gisella Geltrich-Ludgate

Geltrich von Sigmarshofen, in memory of the author's father, Rudolf Karl Geldreich
1904–1981
(published by Creative with Words Publications, 1985)

Ruth Margarete Geldreich, née Boehnke, in memory of the author's mother, Ruth Margarete Geldreich, née Boehnke
1910–1989
(published by Creative with Words Publications, 1994)

Gold Child Urle: Ursula Ingrid Kristensen, née Geldreich, 1935–2001, in memory of the author's sister
(published by Creative with Words Publications, 2001)

Tales and Bedtime Stories
(published January 18, 2013, by Xlibris)
Library of Congress Control Number: 2012923853

The Muddy Little Bell
(published May 9, 2013, by Xlibris)
Library of Congress Control Number: 2013905477

The Lucia Rider
(published November 18, 2013, by Xlibris)
Library of Congress Control Number: 2013918730

Stepping through Time
(published May 12, 2014, by Xlibris)
Library of Congress Control Number: 2014906340

Fathers Can Be Good Dads
(published September 25, 2014, by Xlibris)
Library of Congress Control Number: 2014914297

Dance around the Treasure Box
(published February 20, 2015, by Xlibris)
Library of Congress Control Number: 2015901808

Two Summers of Adjustment
(published December 28, 2015, by Xlibris)
Library of Congress Control Number: 2015921174

The Little People of Oakcreek
(published April 23, 2016, by Xlibris)
Library of Congress Control Number: 2016906328

Cindy the Balcony Cocoon
(published May 27, 2016, by Xlibris)
Library of Congress Control Number: 2016908513

Out of Balance
(published 2016 by Xlibris)
Library of Congress Control Number: 2016915352

Stories, Tales, Folklore, and Such As!
(published 2016 by Xlibris)
Library of Congress Control Number: 2017900063

Jet the Cat
(published April 6, 2017, by Xlibris)
Library of Congress Control Number: 2017904990

Gedichte eines Lebens (Poetry through a Lifetime)
Part I: Early Years (with English translations by the author)
(published August 23, 2017, by AuthorHouse)
Library of Congress Control Number: 2017911409

Poetry through a Lifetime
Part II: Later Years
(published March 9, 2017, by AuthorHouse)
Library of Congress Control Number 2017911409

Let Us Celebrate the Season!
(Published October 17, 2018, by AuthorHouse)
Library of Congress Control Number 2018912305

There Were Many of Us on Three Continents—
Memoirs of Brigitta Gisella Geltrich-Ludgate and Her Family
Volume I
(From Author's birth to Canadian Years)
(published by Creative With Words Publications, 2019/2020.)

There Were Many of Us on Three Continents—
Memoirs of Brigitta Gisella Geltrich-Ludgate and Her Family
Volume II
(From Canadian Years to Author's Retirement)
(published by Creative With Words Publications, 2020/2021.)

Ferdy and Irene
(Still being prepared)

Moving to Alaska
(Still being prepared)

One Two Three Stories in One
(published by AuthorHouse, 05/16/2022)
ISBN 978-1-6655-5975-1

Caressing Me As I Grow Old!
(Poetry)
(Still being prepared)

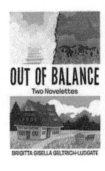

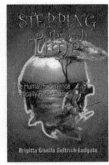

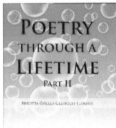

Printed in the United States
by Baker & Taylor Publisher Services